When My Nib Speaks

(Scatters Ink Aloud In 25 Differnet Genres)

Published By

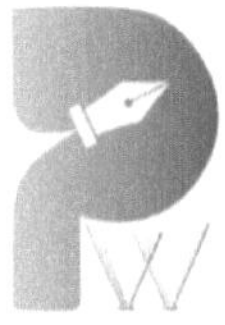

When My Nib Speaks

(Scatters Ink Aloud In 25 Differnet Genres)

Inked By

Thahaseen M. Hussain

ABOUT THE AUTHOR

Dr.Thahaseen, a twenty two year old introverted dentist who became a writer. Writing made people know me, as I hardly speak out to people. All my views and thoughts gets reflected just through my words. I chose to speak through my ink to this world. I hope it replies me back.

ABOUT THE BOOK

The book is purely about my life experiences of the past years. The lessons I learnt from my failures, when I started living alone for the first time and the different struggles from society and people around, the various memories and views on how the world should be and wished to be. It depicts the life of every introverted girl who was the most pampered at home and had to leave home after school, who also loves to travel the world.

<u>INDEX</u>

Why?

THE PAST IS LONG DEAD

Don't search for yesterday's clouds in today's

sky

NOTHING IS PERMANENT

Have you seen any leaves that has not dried at all?

Then, why do you bother or worry when the flowers

wilt?

<u>WHY DOES THE SKY CRACK?</u>

For the wings to get entangled

Or

For the wings to fly high to different skies?

<u>"THE STANDARD BOOK OF SPELLS"</u>
<u>-BY MIRANDA GOSHAWK: EDITION-</u>
<u>1234567...</u>

Inky-pinky-ponky is not working,

Did the spells change now?

How will I get a solution to the confused decisions

of my life?

<u>THE BALANCE BETWEEN THE SMILE AND TEARS</u>

DESTINY-

People called when they didn't know why,

But was always a gobbledgook for me,

Have I reached my destiny now?

Or is it a trial?

To make me understand,

Wider the smile

More the

TEARS.

<u>SERENDIPITY VERSUS DESTINY</u>

We have prayed the most, during our results,

No wonders happened so far, till today,

Yet, wishing for miracles to happen.

"The first prize goes to -"

Our expectations well up

Serendipity sending showers.

Who won?

DESTINY!

<u>DOUBT WHO HAS THE STEARING: CAR DRIVER OR THE HAND-CARTER</u>

Wisely alert the car driver

Mirage of stearing he sees in hand cart

Directs: MOVE, RIGHT AND REVERSE...

Feminism

<u>FEMINISM</u>

Gender doesn't owe anyone any slavery coins

<u>THE SURNAME MATTERS</u>

The world remembers - Marie Curie, Sunitha Williams,

Indira Gandhi, Kiran Bedi.

But forgot (Didn't want to know as well) - Marie

Sklodowska, Sunitha Pandey, Indira.P. Nehru, Kiran

Peshawaria.

Acknowledge her with her birthname to make her proud.

<u>RUN TILL YOU SUCCEED</u>

My dreams are like the colourful butterflies

And I'm the little child running behind it

<u>AFTER EVERY FAILURE</u>

Reset, readjust, restart, refocus

whenever life laughs at you

<u>RISE UP LADY</u>

LOSS

Life's laboratory,

Leads your path,

Lesser your sluggish laziness,

Lengthier victory catalogue will be.

Learn from your nudiustertian night's tears.

Lady of dreams - you aren't defeated within,

Laminate your presence, design your own law LIST.

FAILURE:TUITION FEE FOR SUCCESS

Distant from kakorrhaphiophobia

Drop your inner insecurities

Demon it is

Dries, chokes confidence's neck

Devote your trust

Decode the magic better

Dumb you dumps

Dare the game wisely.

<u>WORK HARDER THAN YESTERDAY</u>

Once the rivers reached the ocean,

There's no coming back.

Never regret your past.

Work for your dreams.

Taking screenshots won't make you a

photographer.

<u>THE DETERMINED ATTEMPT</u>

Survive

Work hard,

For your journey

Which you dreamt of.

Don't declare victory at halfpace.

Kill your overconfidence at its root,

Taking screenshots won't make you a

photographer.

Try, strain, struggle, cope, strive, aim and achieve.

FEAR OF FEAR

Fear always puts a rope onto the neck of self-esteem

& chokes the confidence and strangles the

insecurities.

THE WINNER

Optimist – Failed

Pessimist - Failed

Realist - Failed

Opportunist - Always succeeded

Open letters

<u>DEAR PAST MISTAKES</u>

You never stopped teaching me

The world appreciates me now.

People who critisized when I failed are now celebrating me.

Thank you so much.

Love,

Success

<u>DEAR 10-YR OLD ME</u>

You had the best time management.

You knew when to study, to play, to watch TV, to

fight with your brother, to paint.

You were more organised than me.

You were never addicted to the worldly pleasures.

I miss you,

I spoiled you.

With guilt,

The Older You.

<u>A LETTER TO A STRICT DAD</u>

Abba,

From

First Rejection, then criticism & finally

acceptance

"தேடிச் சோறுநிதந் தின்று – பல சின்னஞ்
சிறுகதைகள்பேசி...**நான் வீழ்வே னென்று
நினைத் தாயோ?**"

اقرأ بسمتي ربيكة اللدزي خلاق

to many many lessons in all languages you always

taught.

To many many mistakes of mine you

corrected from discipline to subjects to life. Lessons

in my life are all growing so well in height, weight

and is also being well expressed everywhere, when

I'm in trouble or when I really need a support, the lessons always stood my way.

And they were always right, even when I've argued it wrong when you taught me.

You have always proved strict parenting with small doses of pampering always worked better than over pampered parenting.

And, when Ammy turned meow and sometimes even by her name; Abba always remained Abba with all respect.

From,

Your favourite child who abided all the rules

<u>DEAR MAYBE</u>

Maybe someday, please become a magic spell like "Maybemora patronum" and let any wish told with 'maybe' come true.

"Maybe" all my 'Wish list' and 'Add to cart products' of Flipkart that are kept for long, come home without paying.

Waiting for wonders to happen,

(MAYBE)

Happy

Wappy

Philosophies

<u>SURVIVAL OF THE FITTEST</u>

DARWIN ON EARTH: The strongest adapting one

of the species will survive.

DARWIN FROM HEAVEN: The one who can

manage to live without phone signal can survive.

Not everywhere, you will get everything you want,

Even the Heaven lacks a good phone signal.

ADAPT, ACCEPT, SURVIVE.

DON'T SHOW OLDAGE HOMES TO THE ONES WHO SHOWED YOU THE WORLD

Made, brought up, nourished you, but was sent to

old-age homes.

Ironically, you forgot and diagnosed them with

Alzheimer's disease

PLANNED SELFLESSNESS WON'T BRING GREATNESS

Don't show off your 'selflessness' and expect

people, to praise you for being 'selfless'

This will be the most cunning form of 'selfishness'

<u>TAKE OFF THE MASK</u>

Minutes

May pass.

Midst the chaos,

Mild smiles work miles.

Malposed selfies are magic memories.

Miracles happen when an agelast smile.

Manually switch off your boring mannequin mode,

March towards colours and stop being colourblind.

<u>PURCHASE HAPPINESS AS</u>
<u>GUIDANCE</u>

If you had bitten your cheek or tongue

accidentally or even had a tooth extraction,

However deep you get a cut on your oral cavity, it

leaves no scars.

It becomes smooth, pink and soft all over again

and again.

It's too, very positive in recovering back

Unlike us,

Shattered and worried after every silliest sorrows be

it:

Marks and ranks,

When the conversation with your best friend gets

reduced day by day,

The deadliest- When you come to know that your

mother is saving the maida atta at home for your

brother, to make him parottas when he comes

home and gives you wheat chappathi instead.

(P.S : My mother secretly loves her son more than

me)

DIFFERENTIATE AND TRANSFORM

Do you know who will rush to your funeral immediately, immaterial of a very important work and circumstances? - Your parents, family and fewer than fewest of your first circle relatives and friends.

"Give your time, your presence,laugh with them, be you in front of them"

For those whom you feel will turn up to your funeral for sure, but may be after their job is done or will visit your house on that weekend or anytime when they are free in that month.

"Give your presence but only in the name of

humanity and nothing beyond, don't act with

sugary dialogues, just smile to them"

And for those who will celebrate your death

"It's more than perfect to be a witch to them from

now on"

There is no Tom, Dick and Harry on the
planet waiting to certify you for being good.

"Live your life, Choose your people"

LOSE THINGS TO KNOW IT'S VALUE

ME too! I said merrily,

To search the lost pot of treasure.

Treasure isn't treasure unless lost.

THE HAPPY EXISTENCE

Love everything around,

From ancient to modern,

From classic to contemporary.

School

<u>LONG LOST LESSONS</u>

"A name or a place should always start with a

capital letter" – our school taught us.

Now in the world ruled by social media,

A hashtag in front of them can break the rule.

"delhi" is wrong , #delhi is perfect

It's okay if we write btwn, tmrw, spl...

But we still find it odd when "i" is written instead

of "I"

But it's okay to see our names starting with the

small letter on Instagram

We lost our long learnt lessons and it's okay now,

While margining the page before writing became

stupid, a talk on lost lessons will seem childish

-thahaseenmhussain

(It's not a sin anymore to write this way)

<u>YOU DON'T NEED YOU VOICE BOX</u>
<u>TO TALK EVERYTIME</u>

"I need pin-drop silence," said the teacher

The last page of the notebook of two friends made

the loudest noises.

<u>TIC TIC VERSUS LUBB DUBB</u>

TIME

Tic tic

To lubb dubb

They danced in rhythm,

The gloom and doom reduced,

There was immense euphoria and peace,

Till heart ran race with an announcement,

'The exam will start in just few minutes'

50

Hostel

THE CRYING HOSTELLER

I was that child who was always excited to leave

home.

Now I'm the same child within, crying a little

everytime, I left home.

THE HOSTEL ROOMS

Every hosteller is never single,

They are always in a blood relationship with

mosquitoes.

<u>HOMEAWAY PHENOMENON</u>

Age is directly proportional to the distance between

your home and hostel

As like every other phenomenon, it has it's own

exceptions and applies only to the people who fall

in the above category.

Medico-life

<u>HOW UNLUCKY ARE YOU?</u>

I came to know I hated the smell of blood after

joining medicine

<u>THE ANATOMY OF CLEANLINESS</u>

Don't just fold your bedsheets,

Also fold your gyri and sulci well.

More the folds, more neat and organized the place

becomes – Both the room and the brain.

<u>LIFE OF A MEDICO</u>

Life was very easy when

PBM meant Paneer Butter Masala

It became tougher when

PBM meant Physics, Biology, Math

It's the toughest and messier when

PBM means Physiology, Biochemistry and

Medicine

58

Painful

truth

<u>STATUTORY WARNING</u>

DISCLAIMER: Emotional dependency is injurious

to health...

(Be it friends, family or any living or a dead

human)

<u>HAVE A COLOURFUL LIFE, BUT</u>
<u>DON'T CHANGE COLOURS</u>

Either bad or good,

Black or white,

The grey shades are falling hard on the eyes.

Chameleons change less colours than humans do.

AT THE END OF A WORD WAR

All we need is an ear that can,

Not just hear but also understand from our

perspective atleast once in a 100 attempt.

-   From a tired daughter, sister and also a friend

sometimes who was never understood.

THE BITTER TRUTH

"Truth alone triumphs", "सत्यमेव जयते" and

"வாய்மையே வெல்லும்" were the best

taught lie from childhood.

Equity, righteousness, honesty will also follow.

CERTAIN VIEWS NEVER CHANGE PSYCHOLOGICALLY

There is no point in consoling your child

who lost his competitive exams with sugar coated

words, who was once punished for scoring low in

his school tests when he was 7yrs old.

Parents may change but the child's view of

approaching failure didn't.

NO TRUST- NO BETRAYAL

Reverse of all holy philosophies

Bliss unfurled when I stopped trusting

And no enemies hurted me.

<u>THE RHYME OF LIFE</u>

Regret – Threats

Hurt – Bursts

Sad you = Mad you

RHS= TBM (Time bomb)

RHS ≠ LHS

Problem left unanswered and unsolved.

Hence,

Mad you = Bad you

Money

FEE STRUCTURE FOR A PRIVATE COLLEGE IN INDIA

Merit seat: 2+2

Recommendations: 2×2

Management seat: 2^2

All are just the same, but in different forms and figures.

Grow up parents...

COSTLY ERRORS

Criminal waste of time without studying will ask

for a big ransom of money as penalty later

Adulthood

<u>ADULT HOOD</u>

Struggling to find a middle ground between the

priorities

<u>INTOVERT</u>

Fights the battle between two words "alone" and

"lonely"

<u>THE DINNER RESPONSIBILITY</u>

From

       "Mom is calling all of you for dinner"

To

       "All come have dinner"

              I grew up.

Friendship

<u>DES VÙ</u>
(The awareness that this will become a memory)

The call I got from my friend of primary school

which I left uninformed,

When your friend of middle school recognizes you

in public and takes you home,

When your high school friend made other know

that I talk too much,

When your friend from college shared your plate of

food every single time even when you had the most

contagious disease,

I know picture perfect that these moments will stay

as a great memory, but the people will remain too.

<u>LIFE TRIANGLE</u>

WhatsApp allows only 3 pinned chats...

It knows the real meaning of Life's triangle

Maybe...

<u>EVOLUTION AND</u>
<u>TRANSFORMATION</u>

Signs your best friend is becoming a stranger:

Rose

Rosh

Roshini

Roshini College

Your phone contact says it all...

<u>THE 10YR GAME</u>

2010 - I lost my friends because of "ME"

2020 - I lost "ME" because of my friends

<u>OVER DEPENDENCY MAY SPOIL FRIENDSHIPS TOO</u>

LOST in care's rain shower

No umbrella could control my over dependency

Care is louder than SILENCE.

PEOPLE LEAVE IN THE HOUR OF NEED

You are a trained pro in consoling, motivating,

appreciating and in wiping tears of people around

you...

So, do it with you too when you are low...

Because, people around you will suddenly get busy,

filled with troubles and get sick 'only when you

terribly need them'

Self Love

<u>SELF GRATITUDE VERSUS</u>
<u>SELFISHNESS</u>

When "Being selfless" and "Being too much

available to people" hurts you,

Never regret to be selfish.

Feed your presence to the little child in you.

Never mind talking to yourself everyday.

Little Thachu needs Thahaseen,

Some little Ammu or Pappu will need you too.

<u>PRIORITISE 'YOU'- NEVER WRONG</u>

Me: People talk to themselves

Me: Really!!

How wierd?!!

Life To Inanimate Objects

THE MOON UNITES

The moon feeds the hungry stomach

Be it Eid or Karwa chauth.

Just the size of the moon differs - a crescent and a

full moon.

Religion: 0

Nature: 1

QUILL IS AN OLD BROKEN WING

LIST

Let flow

List your emotions

Let quill cry ink

Leak on quire her tears

Lay down her voices through letters

Lake of thoughts, she had to say!

Let quill fly again with words this time!

<u>PERISHED PEACE</u>

84

SILENCE was ruined thoroughly throughout by the

lifeless cellphone with non-stop ting-ting noises

made

<u>THE THREE LEGGED BEING</u>

The charmingly spinning three legged being

With outstretched fluttering wings that cannot fly

joyfully,

Encounters a string of people with contrasting

minds

Some heavenly minded, some envious souls,

Some guiltless creatures, some cruel hearts

Is invariably unclear with people's errands

The ignorant being with a head and three wings

Didn't know that humans are poles apart from

each other

He always rotated clockwise for right minded

And counter clockwise for the wicked

But neither of the people were truly righteous

For the hybrids: The bad in good souls and good in

bad witches

The fan started swirling either way

But never stopped gifting virtuous air

But the fan was still for a day

This time with a head, three wings and a rope

With a hopeless human in it

Questioning himself for the episode

But next morning, served its purpose of giving air

To these dissimilar and selfish mindeds

Little did the higgledy-piggledy ignorant being

knew

That the array of shades man has, cannot be

Understood by another human himself

Always presented good and blessed air everytime

he was switched on!

<u>THE DIAMOND FLIGHT</u>

Screamings and buzz with joy,

Ignoring the life on earth.

Just to catch sight of me-

The quadrilateral me-The kite

Gaze at me: Humankind

Stop looking straight for a while

Until the child holding me leaves me,

Until I fly away and beyond the clouds.

Look high up the sky!

Cry your worries, it'll fly away with me,

Make a wish, it'll fly heights with me.

My fuel air is polluted, I care not,

I fly without wings

In the breezy wild winds.

Care not your troubles,

Fly beyond skies!

Take a ride on me,

I'm not the flying carpet

But I call myself "The Aircab"

Pong pong:Come with me

World is wide but not

Wider than our wishes

Let's take wings and fly together zzzing zzing.

Hunger

<u>STARVATION – MOTHER OF MODERN CRIME</u>

BLIND- No issues,

Blind mind always is!

Beverage tittynope left-

Best drink during starvation,

Bowl of food,

Breeds happiness in hunger.

Bandage bleeding stomach,

Burn your closed FIST!

<u>RAIN, RAIN: DON'T GO AWAY</u>

Achieve

Overcome starvation

Cry with me

She begged the clouds

Brontide elsewhere provoked her hopes

The dark sky gave her warmth

Drinking her tears didn't quench her thirst

She is not ready for the heavenly sip

Food

<u>MY CRYING TONGUE</u>

TEARS well up not just with sorrowful events,

Sometimes, they roll down with happiness too!

But the scrumptious looking brown lady

Who is dressed with nuts

Made my tastebuds cry

Passionately and intensely!

Everytime I

PERCEIVE

<u>DECORATE YOUR TUMMY</u>

SIP

The coffee☕

Hallmark jentacular beverage!

Bathe your empty stomach

Dress with bread and porridge

Give her a juice face wash

Protect the pretty lady from the molesters

Hide her from the evil demon: WEIGHT LOSS

INDIAN PARENTS LOGIC

The more unpleasant the taste of food is

The more green it looks

The more healthier it would be

How absurd?!?!

Passion

<u>THE WAR</u>

An unwelcomed profession turned shameless with

a steady, strong, slapping shot from her loving

passion

Confused And A Betraying Mankind

RED DEPICTS TRADITION OR
DANGER

PERCEIVE the differences between an angel and

beldam

Both appear extremely similar whenever we look,

Water can make a cripple float

And can also drown you

Beware of everything around

Flavour - Odour - Colour

Interpret shades,

SURVIVE!

BITTER AND A SWEET HUMAN
INNOCENCE

Sorrow and happiness

Crowded and lonely

Are Broken and whole

With pain and joy

Sometimes with all the above, all at once dancing

over within

Homo sapeins are never pleased with one.

Over complicated pitiful Greedy sapiens they will

remain!

<u>WHEN WILL WE BE GRATEFUL?</u>

The faultless moon & the pitch dark sky

Amazed by the elegance of their fond child: Pearl

She resembled the moon, voiced the dark sky

Aware & alerted in maintaining silence & tranquility,

For Pearl & her boon companions to sleep with peace.

Every morning ,the moon requested the blue sky:

"Take care of my toddler, Pearl in my absence".

The blue sky speechless, agreed to the moon

But she knew moon never had a child!

The mother queen blue sky was as busy as a bee

Solacing her angry King: The Sun

King Sun annoyed by the hustle & bustle made

By the folks of the dynasty: mankind

The fuss made by the humanity were unholy.

The displeased king punished the folks;

He dried the dynasty as dry as a bone,

He set fire to the trees,

The kingdom had neither food nor water.

The ignorant moon & the dark sky,

Not knowing the punishments given by the king

Came with zeal to meet their daughter,

But ,for their dismay, Pearl was missing.

They looked her in every spot.

Far & wide, near & far, high & low

Here& there & everywhere-She was missing.

The agonised parents moaned to the king:Sun

The mighty sun agreed to find their child,

But urged the moon not to keep the dynasty

Calm at night for their ungrateful deeds.

The pious moon never admitted, She said:

"It is my duty to look after her daughter's friends!"

The provoked sun:" What about the adversity they made,

To ruin my green kingdom?"

The bowed down moon, apologized:"It was the tantrums

Made by her child & her friends while playing

And promised to make the dynasty greener than green

Awestruck by the moon's ignorance & gratefulness,

The sun's anger hacked down.

The sun gave food & water to the ungrateful creatures.

The dynasty was fortunate with their needfulness.

That night the lovely parents found their daughter,

Pearl was asleep over the dazzling grey waters

The blue sky recognized that Pearl was not true,

But just the Reflection of the moon on the night's water

The worried blue sky cried hearts out; raining

To clean the dynasty to people of the world

Still the unworthy people, enjoyed rains

Added plastic trash, wrappers & many more

Supplementing filth to the beautiful kingdom.

We though aware of the harm we make, are still

Irresponsible to rebuild the dynasty;

But always wanted the imaginary chore of the moon

For a squeaking clean & green kingdom: THE EARTH!!

God

GOD'S DREAM

Too many wishes; Too many requests;

Too many threats; Too many blames,

Enough of all the greedy wishes,

I need a needless audience yet thankful ones.

Can't you all see I scream my lungs out in the name of

thunder

And cry my hearts out in the form of rains.

Calm down: Give your greediness a pause.

"Why me? " was never asked whenever you won,

But always asked every time you lost.

A world of people whose only wish is

"For the ink to stay in an unfilled ink pen,

Till the end of the exam" is always better than

A want for the pricely possessions.

A prayer of changing the definition of balanced food

To chocolate in one hand and icecream cakes in other

Than a sadistic wish of befalling of your enemy

Remember the wish of a blind man to see is like

A bookmark and the last page of the book.

So, if you can't be thankful, at least don't blame.

I know everything you are about to tell me

Yet "I listen and will keep listening"

I made you and I'll adorn you with all the beauty of the

world.

Children of the greedy globe: Calm down

And handle 'Plan B' of every phase of life in your own way.

Stay raw and real without jealousy

And stay happy with your own non upgraded existence!!!

<u>IF GOD TURNS POSSESSIVE</u>

Why are these people not spending time with me??

Even when they do,

MY man whom I made is crying to ME about some

other human sitting in MY planet

Should I feel jealous of my own people?

Ocean

BEGGED FORGIVENESS

The sea waves apologized repeatedly by touching

her feet

THE OCEAN

How big, how blue, how beautiful!

Travel

HILL STATIONS

When the cold can warm your heart!!

THE EXPLORER

A nomad I will remain for my whole life: In love

with distance and uncharted places...

THE NOMADIC MEASUREMENTS

Life is short, but the world is wide!

<u>SEPARATED BY 363 DAYS</u>

Dec 31-11:59 pm and

Jan 1-12:00am

Are like bookmarks and the last page of a novel...

They come so close to meet each other but couldn't,

in the same year...

<u>THE HEAVEN IS WITHIN</u>

Where the thrilling clouds embrace the hills with

Love, we mortals call it heaven.

<u>PHOTOS: RETURN TICKET TO MEMORIES</u>

FIST your troubles

Find your old photographs,

For nothing changed

Far off years passed.

From peristeronic palaces

Fauna graced green gardens

Fabulous they remain

Fixed, fond and DISTANT!

Wish

DEATH: A BEAUTIFUL GIFT

I wish, I die with my family on the same day, same

time or die before them so that I don't see them

die...

Tsunami killed a family on the shore the

newspaper read, the next day...

"Have you ever believed that tsunami could be

some answered prayers of a little girl?!?!"

WISH

What you are looking for is one call away is a myth!

What you are looking for is one prayer away

The Corona Virus

QUIT YOUR ROOMS: BREAK THE DISTANCE

Summer vacation: Failed

Winter vacation: Failed

Family functions: Failed

A 30kb nanoparticle: Successfully united families under the same roof

Waiting for a further smaller virus to come, to unite them in the same room

(Note:KB is not kilobytes, KB is kilobase genome)

EVER DREAMT OF A VACATION AT HOME?

When did you have your last long holiday??

In the academic year COVID 19-20

<u>WATCH THE GAME FROM HOME</u>

Stop finding awe in a warfield...

Our warriors are fighting with lathi, guns,

injections and medicines...

Don't get shot by coming in the way of the bullet

which was aimed at the Criminal Corona

Stay home

Stay safe

<u>COME BACK MONDAY</u>

Officers - Forget holidays, you had to work on

'Independence day' too!

Doctors - All day is Monday

Others - All day is 'Happy at home day'!

Students- All day is Sunday

Daily wagers – Ironically, praying for their

Mondays to come, for them to survive!

<u>THE CRYING EARTH</u>

People thought I'm happier than before with no

pollution from industries & vehicles

Actually I'm not...

Cutting my hands(Trees) was less painful

Right now, I'm getting stabbed & dug on different

parts of my body, to bury my own dead children

back in my womb!

Stop killing my kids Mr. Alien Virus

From,

A crying mother!

SALUTE THE HEROES

My dear unwelcomed enemy Mr.Corona,

Keep eating our apples everyday- The doctors are

not going away anytime now...

You will get punished for all the crimes you did

from our officers, serving on the road right now...

You will get swept off into the trash sooner by our

sweepers

Chat Story

<u>THE THREE GENERATION TALKS</u>
<u>(A Chat on the whatsapp group)</u>

Me: I have plans to sell something on OLX

Mom: What do you wanna sell now? Don't you

dare touch my old stuff

Me: Ahhhh... I'm gonna sell your son! I don't need

that annoying creature at home!

Mom: What did he do now? I'm sure you

troubled him someway!

(Granny typing...)

Me: Why do you always support your son?

Granny: Did you upload his picture on OLX?

What's the prize? I would love to buy him at any

cost! Don't mind selling him to me.

Mom: HAHHAHA

Me: Hate you both

Granny: Upload a good picture of his!

Memories

MEMORIES

Some memories are the well cherished ones – to be

told to any new people you meet

Some are crazy – a flash memory of it makes you

laugh

Some are scary, that you see yourself a hero for

having crossed the battle.

Some are buried deep under the dark ocean and

you wish for a time machine to change it someway.

THE MUTED MEMORIES

Some words are not meant to be said or heard,

But just felt and forgotten.